W9-AZS-674

Nat the School Cat

Nat is looking for a home. Some children take him into their school. There he finds the food and love he needs.

Then, one day, the school is dark and the children are gone! What will Nat do?

Here are some new words that you will read in this book:

built .... **made.**
Sam built his house one block at a time.

classroom .... **a room in school, where children learn.**
After school, the classroom was empty.

explored ..... **looked in new places and for new things.**
Grandpa explored the hills.

lonely .... **feeling sad because you are by yourself.**
David felt lonely when his dog ran away.

machines .... **things used to make something or move something.**
Abby used machines to move the rocks.

peered ...... **looked closely.**
Kathy saw many shapes when she peered at the fire.

rumbled ..... **made a low, earth-shaking sound, like thunder.**
Norah felt the room shake as the tractor rumbled by.

visitor .... **someone who comes to see you for a short time.**
Grandma was a visitor for three days.

wondered .... **thought about.**
Max wondered how the sun moved across the sky.

EASY-TO-READ ANIMAL ADVENTURES:

CATKIN the Curious Kitten
LENNY the Lost Donkey
HONEY the Hospital Dog
NAT the School Cat
TOMMY the Timid Foal
DINAH the Dog with a Difference

A Note to Grownups: This delightful "Real Life" animal adventure also introduces young readers to the following themes: loneliness and fear, the security of home, school as a positive experience, and children's relationship to their environment.

On page 28, a section called "Things to Talk About" encourages children to explore these themes with other children and with adults. The questions in "Things to Talk About" also give adults a chance to participate in the learning – and enjoyment – to be found in this story.

Library of Congress Cataloging-in-Publication Data

Napier, Lena.
Nat, the school cat.

(Easy-to-read animal adventures)
Summary: A homeless cat named Nat finds the food and love he needs with a group of children in their classroom at school.
[1. Cats–Fiction. 2. Schools–Fiction] I. Bartram, Haworth, ill. II. Title. III. Series.
PZ7.N14Nat 1985 [E] 85-15909
ISBN 0-918831-23-7 (lib. bdg.)
ISBN 0-918831-48-2

North American edition first published in 1985 by

Gareth Stevens, Inc.
7221 West Green Tree Road
Milwaukee, Wisconsin 53223

First published in Australia by Childerset Pty. Ltd. with an original text copyright by Lena Napier.

Reading Consultant: Libby Gifford
Series Editor: Mark J. Sachner
Designer: Sharon Burris

Typeset by Colony Pre-Press • Milwaukee, Wisconsin 53208 USA

Nat
the School Cat

Story by
Lena Napier

Photography by
Haworth Bartram

Gareth Stevens Publishing
Milwaukee

Nat was lonely. He was hungry, too.

He stood outside the door. He meowed and meowed. But the door stayed shut.

Nat wanted to hear the old woman call, "Food, Nat!"

But no one came. Not for a whole week.

"I must find a new home, " Nat said to himself.

Nat went into town. He found a place
to nap.

When he woke he heard a lot of noise.
Big machines rumbled. Hammers banged.

Nat was scared.

Then the noise stopped. Two men sat down to eat lunch.

"I'm hungry!" Nat remembered. He jumped down.

"Look! We have a visitor," said one man. "And he looks hungry."

The man held out his tuna sandwich. He called, "Here kitty!"

Nat had found some friends!

Every day the men gave Nat food.

After meals, Nat gave himself a bath.
Then he curled up for a nap.

Nat watched his friends at work.

"What are they doing?" Nat wondered.

Then, one day, the men were gone.
They had finished their work.

They had built a new school.

Nat felt lonely again. But soon, children came to the school. They were noisy.

He watched the children, and they watched him.

Later, the children ate lunch. They saw Nat. They talked about him.

"Look at the white cat!"

"Where is his home?"

"He looks hungry."

One girl held out her hand. Nat sniffed at it.

"Do you like peanut butter?" she asked Nat.

Nat took a bite. "This tastes good," he purred.

Then a teacher came out. She said, "Don't feed that cat. It won't go home if you do."

Nat felt sad. He had no home.

Nat stayed near the school. Each day, the children fed him. Soon they asked the teacher, "May we keep him? Please?" At last the teacher said, "O.K."

The teacher let Nat into the classroom. He looked at the children's artwork. He sniffed the crayons.

Nat had a good time in the classroom. The children loved him. They fed him every day. And they laughed when he played in the yarn box. Nat felt happy again.

Then one day the children did not come to school.

They did not come the next day or the next. All the doors were locked. All the classrooms were dark and empty. And the windows were closed.

Nat missed the children. He was sad. And he was hungry.

Nat got thinner each day. He had no food.

Days passed. He waited and waited. Every day he peered through the window.

Nat got very thin. Then one day, he could not even stand up.

The next day the children came back. They found poor Nat. He looked very sick.

The teacher carried Nat into the school. Nat slept for a long time. When he woke, he saw the children. They fed him. And he felt much better.

Then he explored the classroom. He looked in the fish bowl. The goldfish were still there.

He looked in the mouse cage. The mice were still inside.

And then Nat saw a new box. It had a blanket in it. It was just right for a cat.

Nat tried it. It felt good. The children smiled. They had made a bed for Nat. And he found it on his own.

Nat felt happy. He knew he had a home at last.

nat

Things to Talk About

Reading can be fun. Talking about the stories we read can be fun, too.

Here are some questions about the story of Nat, the school cat. Now is your chance to talk about how you feel about the story. If you like, show these questions to a grownup you know. He or she will be happy to talk about the questions with you. Now you can have fun reading <u>and</u> talking about Nat and his adventures!

1. When Nat has no home, he feels sad. Why do you think he feels this way?

2. What makes <u>you</u> feel lonely and sad?

3. When Nat meets the workers and children, he feels happy. What sorts of things make <u>you</u> happy?

4. How do the children at school show Nat that they love him?

5. How do you show others that you care about them?

6. Here are what we call the five senses: sight, hearing, smell, taste, and touch. In the story, what does Nat see, hear, smell, taste, and feel?

7. What is your favorite thing to hear? What do you <u>least</u> like to hear?

8. Look at pages 12 and 13. Here, Nat sees a new building being built. Ask a grownup you know to take you to watch a new building going up. Can you guess what it will be or what it will look like when it is done?

9. Look at pages 4 and 5 and pages 22 and 23. Nat sees buildings that are dark and locked up. What do you think about when you see a dark, empty building?

10. Nat likes coming to school. But school is also Nat's home. When you leave home to come to school, how do you feel?

11. What animals are allowed in your school? What are not? Why aren't they allowed?

12. School is a fun place for Nat. Do you have fun with your friends at school? What do you do that is fun at school?

13. Nat always learns things at school. He learns about crayons and art and fish and mice. What things do you like to learn about at school?

14. Nat felt bad when the school was closed for a while. But the children came back, and the teachers came back, and Nat came back. Do you ever feel bad about school? What makes you feel bad? And what makes you feel good again?

15. Can you remember what school was like when you first went there? How is it different for you now?

16. Look at the list of New Words on page 1. Can you find these words in the story? Use the Index of New Words on page 30. Can you think of new ways to use these words?

Index of New Words

More Easy-to-Read Animal Adventures that are fun to read and talk about:

Catkin the Curious Kitten

Sometimes Catkin's curiosity gets her into trouble. But she learns how to be careful. And then her curiosity helps her find out all kinds of things!

Dinah the Dog with a Difference

Dinah is different from the other puppies. Her mother is worried. But being different is not so bad. In fact, it makes her just right for a very special job!

Honey the Hospital Dog

Honey is a very special dog – a hospital dog! With her help, everyone learns how important it is to have good friends.

Honey gets lots of love, too. And she keeps an eye out for trouble!

Lenny the Lost Donkey

Lenny follows the children to school one day. On the way, he gets lost. He soon finds out how important good friends are.

And he finds out that school is not the only place for learning about things!

Tommy the Timid Foal

Tommy finds it hard to make friends. "What good are friends?" he asks.

Then he meets some animals and a young boy. And he finds out that having friends isn't so bad after all!